Climb that hill. Who cares if you slip?

Dream when you can. Let magic rip!

Get up and fly; it's not too late

Grab that dream before it escapes.

You bad fairy! Be the best there is

Make things happen! Give the world some fizzzzz!

—SO

To Annie, my own spike-haired, rat-heel booted bad fairy

—MC

Flax the feral Fairy

Tiffany Mandrake

Illustrated by Martin Chatterton

LITTLE HARE
www.littleharebooks.com

Little Hare Books
8/21 Mary Street, Surry Hills
NSW 2010 AUSTRALIA

www.littleharebooks.com

First published in 2009
Reprinted in 2009 (twice)

National Library of Australia
Cataloguing-in-Publication entry

Mandrake, Tiffany.

Flax the feral fairy / Tiffany Mandrake;
illustrator, Martin Chatterton.

978 1 921272 70 7 (pbk.)

For primary school age.

Fairies—Juvenile fiction.

Chatterton, Martin.

A823.4

Cover design by Martin Chatterton
Set in 16/22 pt Bembo by Clinton Ellicott
Printed in China by WKT Company Limited

7 6 5 4 3

Contents

A Note from Tiffany Mandrake

Psst, this is me, Tiffany Mandrake, speaking to you from my cosy, creepy cottage in the grounds of Hags' Abademy.* This is the story of one bad fairy, named Flax Lilykicker. I promised not to tell anyone about Flax . . . but you can keep a secret, can't you?

Sure you can.

Remember, not a word to anyone!

*An abademy is a place where bad fairies go to study Badness.

1. Hags in the Glen

Two water hags* sat on a rotten log in a
Scottish glen. Their names were Maggie
Nabbie and Auld Anni. Scottish water
hags wear a lot of shawls and long ragged
skirts, and they always have bare feet.
Their hair is a bit green, like waterweed.

---

*Water hags are fairy breed. The fairy breed are not human.
There are many different kinds.

They are not ugly but there is something about them that makes humans want to leave in a hurry.

Maggie and Anni tossed pebbles into the loch, half-hoping to disturb a loch-monster. They were both bored and discontented.

Maggie had once been called the Hag o' Loch Dread. She had ducked folk in her loch. Anni o' the Glen had danced young men into a swamp on their wedding day. But that was long ago.

'The humans have no respect,' said Maggie, rattling her rabbit-bone necklace.

'No wonder,' said Anni, 'when young fairies flit about, doing sweet deeds. Who can respect that?'

'Even boggarts and trolls scarcely bother humans today.' Maggie sighed. 'Maybe we should give up on humans

completely and go to live somewhere else.'

'Speak for yourself, Hag!' said a cranky little voice from down near Maggie's knee. The creature was a critter-fae.⋆ It looked like a tiny winged dog.

'You can't give up on humans. Humans *need* the fairy breed!' the dog-fae snapped. 'Without us, they'll grow sour and mean.

⋆*A critter-fae is an imp with animal DNA. They are fairy breed.*

They'll get fat and bored, and even sillier than they are now.'

Auld Anni sniffed. 'If a human saw you, it would call for Animal Control.'

'You've gone *soft*,' said the dog-fae. 'No wonder humans have no respect! You hags should set an example to young bad fairies.'

'There *are* no young bad fairies,' said Maggie.

'Nonsense!' said the dog-fae. 'Your old friend Kirsty Breeks has discovered a young bad fairy at Miss Kisses' Academy of Sweetness for Little Fairies.'

'What's our Kirsty doing *there*?' asked Maggie.

'Her loch was drained and now she works as a cleaner,' said the dog-fae.

'As a *what*?' gasped Anni. 'How *could* she?'

The dog-fae ignored this. 'Miss Kisses wants to turn this young bad fairy into a good fairy,' it continued. 'You hags must prevent her. We of the critter-fae will help, but *you* must lead the way.'

Before the hags could answer, the dog-fae scampered into the air and buzzed away.

'Well!' said Maggie. 'Why must *we* do it?'

'Someone has to,' pointed out Anni. 'Otherwise, this young bad fairy will be lost to us.' A faint skirling of bagpipes echoed around the glen. 'Can we let that happen?'

Maggie tightened her shawl. For the first time in years her necklace rattled with glee. 'No, Auld Anni, we cannot.'

The two hags left at once for Miss Kisses' Academy of Sweetness.

2. Miss Kisses' Academy of Sweetness for Little Fairies

Miss Kisses' Academy of Sweetness for Little Fairies stands on a hillside, above a human village. It probably isn't far from where you live, but you won't see it.*

The Academy had thirteen pupils. On one particular morning, twelve of them

---

The fairy breed use special spells, called DNMs—or Don't Notice Me—spells, to make sure you don't.

were putting on pink frocks with extra frills.

'What's going on?' asked Flax, the thirteenth fairy. She had not been at Miss Kisses' Academy for long.

Catkin Summerday smiled. 'There's a party in the Pink Pavilion. Butterfly has earned her Seal of Sweetness.'

Flax put on her hacked-feather skirt with caterpillar stockings and her rat-heeled boots. She hoped there would be food at the party.

'Bluebirds bring invitations to our window,' cooed Catkin.*

Petal Cherrypainter opened the casement windows of Daisy Dorm. 'Here they come!' A flock of pale blue birds swept down. Each held a pink invitation in its beak.

Bluebirds often fly messages for good fairies.

Flax snatched at the fanciest one, but the bird dodged and presented the card to Butterfly Cloudsinger.

Eleven fairies squealed with pleasure. 'Butterfly has her Seal of Sweetness!' they said. 'We love you, Butterfly!'

Smiling, Butterfly flitted away.

Flax elbowed Opal Forestbloom aside and snatched at another invitation. Again, the bluebird avoided her and gave the card to Pearl Shellseeker.

Fairy after fairy received a pink card and danced away to join the party. Off went Bliss Dewsipper and Heather Braeside, then Canary Finchfeather, Opal, Petal, Catkin and all the rest.

Flax was left alone in Daisy Dorm. As the bluebirds flittered towards the trees she leaned out the window. 'Hey, birdbrains! Where's *my* invitation?'

As Flax yelled out, the two hags* approached the Academy of Sweetness and paused outside the window.

'Out of the way!' bawled Flax as a fat, grumpy bluebird swooped towards her.

'Lassie, do you know—' the hags began.

Flax picked up Butterfly's second-best slipper and threw it at Maggie's head. 'Go away, you clackety slopper!'

---

*Scottish water hags can travel anywhere they like.

The bluebird dropped the envelope, and flew away with an angry twitter. 'Come back!' howled Flax. 'Give me that invitation, or you'll regret it!'

Auld Anni picked up the envelope and opened it. *'Miss Kisses informs Flax Lilykicker that she is not—'*

Flax threw a hairbrush at Anni. 'That's my invitation, you tatty old haggis!' She jumped out the window, snatched the card from Anni and raced away.

Auld Anni grinned. 'Flax Lilykicker must be the bad fairy Kirsty discovered.'

Maggie Nabbie rattled her rabbit-bone necklace. 'We must find Kirsty and learn more.' She sniffed, almost choking at the smell of pink bubblegum. But yet . . . she could also smell a trace of pond-slime.

'This way!' said Maggie. The hags followed their noses down to the cellar.

3. Hags in the Cellar

In the dank cellar under the Academy,
Kirsty tended her loch-monster, Vetch.
She had rescued him when her loch was
drained. She chuckled with delight when
the other hags arrived, then exchanged
bony hugs with them. Auld Anni got
misty-eyed.

'What *are* you doing out *here*?' asked
Maggie.

'Miss Kisses fills these wee fairies with sweetness until it seeps out their pores,' said Kirsty. 'I try to add a balance of badness. One hag cannot balance a loch-full of syrup, but one wee bad fairy has come to the place. Meeting her gave me an idea. I want us to start an Academy of our own.'

'For *one* bad fairy?' asked Anni.

'Where there is one, there must be more,' said Kirsty. 'We shall seek them far and wide. Wee ogres, tiny trolls, sulky selkies, mischievous mers, ill-mannered imps. All will be welcome.' She drew herself up. 'The fairy breed must survive in all its wondrous variety! There is a place for sweetness ... but there must also be some badness for balance. Otherwise, who will keep the humans on their toes?'

Maggie and Anni both applauded, and
bagpipes skirled about the cellar. Vetch
the loch-monster raised his head and
hissed with approval.

'We must take only *bad* fairies,' said
Maggie.

'We need some kind of test to be sure,'
agreed Anni. 'The critter-fae can help
with that.'

'Good!' said Kirsty. 'Let's do this quickly. Something tells me wee Flax is about to get in a vat-load of trouble.'

And so, in the cellar below Miss Kisses' Academy of Sweetness for Little Fairies, the Hags' Abademy of Badness was born.

4. Flax is Pinked in the Pavilion

While the hags were hatching their plans in the cellar, Flax was peering through the pink glass of the Pavilion. She saw Butterfly Cloudsinger sitting on a pink throne, with a huge pink brooch★ on her frock.

Then Flax saw the food.

★*This was her Seal of Sweetness.*

'Gooseberry tartlets!' she moaned. 'Hazelnut truffles with jelly! Yum!'

Petal popped her head out from the Pink Pavilion. 'Flax, you're missing the butter suckers! They're yummy.'

Flax dived into the Pavilion, and grabbed a sugar pop. Her fingers closed on air.

She snatched a bowl of blackberry flummery fool. It shimmered and turned to mist in her mouth.

When she lunged for a butter sucker, her favourite sticky treat, it bounced away.

Butterfly floated down and took the invitation from Flax's pocket. She read it aloud. '*Miss Kisses informs Flax Lilykicker that she is **not** invited to the Pink Pavilion for Butterfly's Seal of Sweetness celebration. She should **not** arrive at five past eleven.*

*She will **not** enjoy gooseberry tartlets,
hazelnut truffles, sugar pops, butter suckers,
and blackberry flummery fool with the rest
of Daisy Dorm.'*

There was a shocked silence, then
Butterfly giggled.

'What's so funny?' said Flax.

'Miss Kisses is *sooo* funny,' said
Butterfly. 'She sent you an *un*-vitation!'

Flax snatched Butterfly's wand and trampled it under her rat-heeled boots.

'What *have* we here?' Miss Kisses arrived in a flurry of silken wings. Her slippers hovered just above the floor as she pointed her pink-tipped wand at Flax.

'Flax dear, you *must* try to be sweet,' Miss Kisses cooed. 'Butterfly earned her Seal of Sweetness by working very hard, and I *know* you will do the same one day! I feel it *here*,' she explained, gently tapping her bosom. 'But, Flax, I have been right through my Fairy-Reporter.★ It lists all the sweet deeds my pupils do. I can't find a record of a sweet deed with your name on it this week. Not one!'

★*A Fairy-Reporter is a magical book that helps fairy breed teachers keep track of their pupils. It notes down deeds, good and bad.*

'That's because I'm a *bad* fairy!'
protested Flax.

'There is no such thing,' said Miss Kisses.
'We used to think bad fairies were born
bad. Now we know that's not so. With
help, bad fairies can be sweet! There are
lots of sweet deeds we can do for humans.'

'What good does that do you?' growled
Flax. 'The humans won't even see you.'

'Sweet deeds lead to a Seal of
Sweetness,' said Miss Kisses. 'Girls, form a
fairy ring. Flax must be pinked★ at once.'

The twelve fairies joined hands and
danced round Flax. She sneezed as thick
pink mist poured from Miss Kisses' wand
and wrapped around her head.

★*Being pinked is one of the worst things that can happen to a
bad fairy. To them it is like someone dying your hair bright
yellow, plastering lipstick all over your face and pouring runny
lime jelly and tinned mushrooms over your favourite shirt.*

Just as Flax was sure she would turn into a puddle of pink sugar, Calla Meadowskipper squealed and fluttered out of the ring.

'What is it, Calla, dear?' cooed Miss Kisses.

'*Ooh! Uggy! Ick!*' Calla pointed to a puddle of slime that oozed from the pavilion floor.

Miss Kisses clicked her tongue. 'What a mess! Off you go, fairies. Back to the dorm. *Kiss-Kiss!* Talk later!'

Twelve fairies flitted away, carrying plates of party treats. Flax tried to follow the food, but Miss Kisses caught her.

'*Kir—sty!*' cried Miss Kisses.

Kirsty Breeks, summoned from the cellar, stamped through the door in her big bare feet.

Miss Kisses smiled. 'This little fairy has

made a mess. See that she cleans it up.'

'I didn't do it,' said Flax, but Miss Kisses turned and skimmed away.

Flax kicked the slime with her rat-heeled boot and glared at the hag. 'Did you make this stuff?'

'Aye. I thought it might save you from a pinking. And if you keep kicking it, you will spoil your frock,' said Kirsty.

'What frock?' Flax looked down, and howled with disgust as she remembered she had been pinked. Instead of her hacked-feather skirt, she now wore a puffy pink fairy frock with a frilly hem and a pattern of tiny pink cross-stitched kisses over her caterpillar stockings.

'Get this pinking spell off me!' yelled Flax.

'I have a message for you.' Kirsty tapped her foot. More slime oozed from the floor.

It smelled of wild moors and mulch. 'At midnight tonight, you will get an invitation.'

'But—'

'You'll get an explanation to go with it. Now flit away, little fairy,' said the hag. She waved her hand and the ooze on the floor was gone.

In the Daisy Dorm the other fairies were writing in their Sweet Deed Books before afternoon lessons. They stared as Flax dragged off the puffy pink frock and climbed into bed, rat-heeled boots and all.

'You can't sleep in the daytime, Flax!' twittered Calla.

'Yes I can,' said Flax, and did.

5. Invitation from the Abademy

Flax woke before midnight. Something fluttered above her face. She swatted at the thing and it yelped. A moment later, a set of tiny fangs fastened on Flax's nose. Flax yelped as well and tossed the thing halfway across the dorm. 'Pickled nightshade!' she squawked.

She rolled over and the fangs nipped her left ear.

'Get up!' sniped a voice that sounded like vinegar.

'What?' Flax scrambled up as something rammed a scrunched-up ball of paper into her mouth. *'Ug-ger-uff!'* gulped Flax.

'Sweet!' remarked Vinegar-voice.

Flax spat out the paper. 'I'm *never* sweet!'

'Read it,' said the voice.

Flax stared at the slumbering fairies. 'What's wrong with them? Why aren't they squealing for help?'

'I laced their bedtime sugar-sip with cat-wort,' said Vinegar-voice. 'It's a herb. Cats love it. Why do you think they spend most of their lives asleep?'

Flax, who never let sleeping cats rest in peace, smoothed the paper and stole Petal's pretty pink candle. The rosy glow showed letters staggering across the paper. *'Are you a bad fairy?'* she read. *'Do you relish being really rotten, disturbingly deceitful, and mindbogglingly bad? Answer Yes or No.'*

Flax didn't need to stop and think. 'Yes!' she blurted.

More lines appeared on the paper, and Flax read on. *'If you answered Yes, you may earn a Badge of Badness.'* Flax looked up. 'What's that? How do I do it? Who is this?'

'Get on with it,' said the creature.

Flax scowled. *'Create and perform an act of breathtaking badness. Answer I Will or I Won't,'* she read, glancing again at the strange creature. 'I WILL!' she said. 'When do I start?'

As she watched, more words appeared on the paper. *'You start now. Go forth and be bad. Help will be provided,'* she read.

Flax reached for her clothes, but all she could find was the fluffy fairy frock. It was too cold to go out bare so she dragged it on. She jumped out the window and set off for the village.

'Why not fly?'

The vinegar-voiced creature hovered a toad-leap from her face. It was half the size of a bluebird. It had four legs, a curling fuzzy tail and small floppy ears. It also had a pair of furry wings. It was patched in brown and white.

'What are you?' demanded Flax.

'I am the dog-fae.'★

'What's a dog-fae?'

'I am,' it said. 'I am *the* dog-fae, the only one of my kind. I am one of the critter-fae.

★*Fae, fetches or imps are all fairy breed. Most of them take pride in being bad.*

You and I are both bad fairies, but I am badder than you.'

'Go away,' said Flax.

The dog-fae buzzed in and bit Flax's nose.

Flax howled and swatted at it but it bounced out of reach with a yelp of glee. '*Yrrrrr*,' it said and showed its teeth. 'Do that again and you're minced fairy.'

'Do *that* again, and you're diced dog-fae!' said Flax. 'Scat! I have bad business in the village.'

'*We* have bad business.' The dog-fae flashed ivory fangs. 'I am your fairy fetch. It is my job to help you earn that Badge of Badness.'

'Why should I need help?'

The dog-fae grinned. 'You can't even fly.'

'Can so.' Sulkily, Flax unfolded her wings. They were limp and small, not like the butterfly sets the other fairies wore.

'You laugh, you die,' she said and leapt into the air.

The dog-fae looped and fluttered far above the fairy's head, giggling shrilly.

Flax's rat-heeled boots brushed the path. Her wings swished and swithered through the slots in her pink fairy frock.

She ignored the dog-fae. The night wind
ruffled her kiss-trimmed petticoats,
and her spiky hair. Flax wanted her old
clothes back but Miss Kisses' pinking
spell was too strong.

6. Dulcinea Sweet

'What's the plan?' asked the dog-fae. The sun had risen, and the fairy and the fetch loitered in the human village.

'I need clothes,' said Flax. She kicked a hole in a garden fence.

'Shouldn't you put on your DNM spell?' said the dog-fae.

'No. I don't care if humans notice me. I want *all* the credit for my bad deeds.'

Flax strolled to a clothes line and stole a pair of green velvet overalls. She had one leg in when she heard a gasp.

A human girl was watching. She had fair hair like Flax's, only longer. In it, she wore a sparkling pink clip. She had a pretty face, like a plastic doll. Flax hated her on sight.

'What are you staring at?' demanded Flax.

'*Ooh!*' The girl clapped her hands. 'You're a fairy! Aren't you *big*?'*

Flax snorted.

'I played a fairy in my last three films,' said the human. 'I had a pretty fairy dress like yours. I had cute little wings too.' She held out her hand. 'I'm Dulcinea Sweet.'

Some people think fairies are invisible because they are small, but most fairies are the same size as you.

Flax put her other leg in the overalls and hauled off the frilly fairy frock. She dragged the straps of the overalls over her shoulders and reached behind to adjust her wings.

'I'm a famous film star,' said Dulcinea, giving up trying to shake Flax's hand. 'I've won four Tiny Treasure Awards for my little fairy roles.' She patted the sparkly clip in her hair. 'This is a present from my biggest fan. Don't you just love it?'

Flax stared at the clip. It was *so* huge and pink. Her nose twitched and her fingers tingled. 'It's magic,' she said. She was surprised.

The clip was a kind of magic, but it didn't smell like fairy breed. Could humans do spells? Flax concentrated on the clip, which seemed to buzz a little tune. *Dulcinea Sweet is here. Dulcinea Sweet is here.*

'*Do* talk to me, fairy!' said Dulcinea. 'I hate this stupid village. I'm bored.'

'Why?' said Flax.

Dulcinea bent close to Flax. 'I'm in hiding. The kidnappers tried to snatch me at an autograph signing!'

'What kidnappers?' asked Flax.

'A man and a woman in a purple van. Mama said if they got me, she'd have to pay lots of money to get me back again.

That's why she's making me hide. Mama says I can't make films until the police catch them,' said Dulcinea. 'People at school call me *Dulci Smith*. The teachers know who I am but they pretend they don't.' She pouted. 'If I don't make a new film soon, the fans will forget me.'

Flax thought Dulcinea was awful but an idea hatched in her mind. She smiled. 'Oooh! How exciting! Tell me *all* about it!' She clasped her hands the way Butterfly Cloudsinger did.

Dulcinea cocked her head. 'Time for school,' she announced. 'I'll tell you later, little fairy.'

Flax crawled out through the fence to where the dog-fae was chasing sparrows.

'Well?' it demanded, staring at the fairy with eyes like crab apple pips.

'I thought of a very bad deed,' said Flax.

'I will kidnap Dulcinea Sweet. Find me a secure place to store a stolen human. Go on. You're my fairy fetch.' She looked hard at the dog-fae, pointed, and said, '*Fetch!*'

The dog-fae circled to get its bearings and peered about. 'One old pink barn with damp straw,' it noted. 'One church with a crumbling crypt. One mouldering mansion built by the Irish madman, O'Connor O'Grady O'Brien.'

The barn was not secure, and the church was infested with tourists, so the mansion was the best choice. It was well out of town and had nasty trees and a gloomy tower. The dog-fae could smell magic.

It was about to find Flax when something caught its attention. A pink van with dark windows was cruising the streets. The dog-fae zipped down for a closer look.

The pink paint on the van was new and streaky. Whoever had painted it hadn't done a good job. It was clear that the van had once been purple.

The dog-fae realised these must be the people who were after Dulcinea Sweet. It sped off to warn Flax that she would have to hurry if she wanted to kidnap the girl herself.

7. Bad Fairy in the School

Meanwhile, Flax put on her DNM spell and perched on the roof of Mama Sweet's car as it headed for the school. When they got there she watched Mama Sweet hand her daughter over to a fierce teacher called Ms Fegmeyer.

Something smelled good. Sniffing hard, Flax followed her nose to the cloakroom and stole the lunches there.

She ate pickles, plums, crunchy things, chewy things, sandwiches, scones and carrots. She drank bottles of fruit drink dry.

She had just finished when the dog-fae sniffed her out. 'Did you find a place to store my human?' she asked.

The dog-fae described the mansion it had chosen. 'You'll have to be quick,' it added. 'Those kidnappers are here in the village. Hurry, or they'll get to Dulcinea first.'

Flax stared hard at a spare banana and turned it rotten. The kidnappers were *here*? What a coincidence! Or ... was it? Were they the ones who had put the spell on the magic clip? Was it calling, telling them where to find Dulcinea Sweet?

'You're wasting time,' said the dog-fae.

'Be quiet. I'm plotting.'

'They—'

Flax grabbed the dog-fae. '*Quiet!*' she snapped. 'When I tell you—*ow!*' She pried the dog-fae's fangs out of her thumb, and stuffed it into her pocket. Then she scowled and plotted, ignoring the high-pitched snarling in her pocket.

After a while, she fished the dog-fae out again. The dog-fae glared at her.

'Pocket me again and you're *mince*, fairy!'

'I've eaten bigger bugs than you,' replied Flax. 'I've decided what I'm going to do. I *was* going to kidnap Dulcinea Sweet and make her mama pay money. *Now* I'm going to save Dulcinea from the kidnappers—'

'That's not a bad deed.'

'*But*,' added Flax, 'after I save her, I'll then kidnap Dulcinea myself. The other kidnappers will get the blame. *I'll* get the money.'

'That's *twisted*!' said the dog-fae.

Flax thought so too.

Her first step was to go to the window of Dulcinea's classroom and cast a Glamour.★

★*This is a spell that makes humans see things that aren't really there.*

As soon as Flax did this, Dulcinea Sweet saw a kidnapper leering through the window. She shrieked and leapt up.

'Please sit down, Dulci.' Ms Fegmeyer disapproved of film stars. She thought they were spoiled and stuck-up. She didn't believe for a moment that anyone had tried to kidnap this one. She thought it was all a publicity stunt.

'*Kidnapper*!' cried Dulcinea, pointing. 'He's after me!'

Ms Fegmeyer stalked to the window. 'Nonsense.'

'He is! He is!' Dulcinea moaned.

Ms Fegmeyer sent her to the sick room.

Flax took off her DNM and tapped on the sick-room window. '*Pssst! Dulcinea!*'

The young film star gasped.

Flax squashed her nose against the glass. 'There's something you should know.'

'What?'

'The kidnappers are in the village.'

'Oh ... oh! I *told* Ms Fegmeyer I saw one of them, but she wouldn't believe me!'

'She doesn't care about you,' said Flax.

Dulcinea's face went grey. Flax fizzed with glee but she kept her face straight. 'I can save you, but you must come *now*!'

'B–b–but ... I have to go to Mama!'

'Give me that clip in your hair,' said Flax. She opened the window.

Dulcinea snatched the clip from her hair and thrust it at Flax. Flax hid it in a clump of stinging nettle for safekeeping.

Dulcinea Sweet is here! it buzzed. *Dulcinea Sweet is here!*

Flax grinned. Very soon Dulcinea Sweet would *not* be here. As Dulcinea scrambled out the window, Flax cast

another Glamour to make it look as if
the little star was asleep in the sick room.
Then she seized Dulcinea's hand. 'I'll
hide you where no one will ever find
you,' she said.

8. The Mouldering Mansion

Hand in hand, the bad fairy and the film star fled from the school, leaving a magic clip behind to fool the kidnappers and a Glamour behind to fool Ms Fegmeyer.

'Can't you fly, fairy?' gasped Dulcinea.

Flax pretended not to hear. The dog-fae sniggered as it clung to her overalls, under her wings.

'Where are we going?' Dulcinea's

chest heaved and her face was a dull red.

'We're escaping the kidnappers,' said Flax. She dragged her victim out of the village. They sped up a stony lane under some mean-looking trees. Between the trees crouched the mouldering mansion,* built of scabby grey stone.

Dulcinea stopped. 'I'm not going in there! There might be ghosts!'

'So what?'

'It's spooky!' whimpered Dulcinea.

Flax skittered up the pocked stone steps that led to the bog-oak door. The dog-fae had chosen wisely. This place looked empty, but something of the fairy breed lurked within.

---

*Mansions, like humans and horses, have personality. If this mansion had been a horse, it would have bucked you off and rolled on you.

Flax dragged Dulcinea through the door and looked for a way to the tower.

'This place gives me a funny feeling,' said Dulcinea.

'Me too,' said Flax. 'I *love* it.'

Inside the mansion was cool and grey. Swags of cobweb hung from chandeliers. The moss-green mats on the floor were

thick with dust. Flax noticed some wide, shallow steps. They led to the next floor. Once they were up there, Flax spotted a crumbling wall that looked promising. Flax kicked it until she discovered a hidden door. 'Through you go,' she ordered Dulcinea.

'N–no—'

Flax crammed the human through the gap. 'Go up into the tower,' she said. 'I'm right behind you!'

Dulcinea snivelled as she shuffled up the cold, winding staircase behind the hidden door. Flax trod on her heels. The dog-fae crawled up to perch on her shoulder. 'There's something ancient and Irish in that tower,' it said.

'Good,' said Flax.

At the top of the stairs, Flax reached around Dulcinea and scrabbled at a door.

There was no latch, but her fingers found a knocker.

Tap-tap-tap! went Flax.

From behind the tower door came a wail. *'Woe to the house of O'Connor O'Grady O'Brien!'*

Dulcinea staggered backwards, treading on Flax's toes. 'But—'

'Close your cakehole.' Flax knocked on the door again. 'Open up!'

'Give me the password first!' wailed the voice.

Flax kicked the door. 'If you don't open up on the count of five, I'll jelly your bones and eat you!'

'Woe, woe to the house of O'Connor O'Grady O'Brien! Woe, woe . . .'

'Five!' yelled Flax. 'Four!'

Dulcinea moaned and fainted at Flax's feet.

'Three-two-one let me in!' bawled Flax.

The door burst open. Flax fell into the tower.

In front of her floated the Irish being. It looked just like a teenage girl who'd forgotten to eat. It wore an old droopy white dress embroidered with shamrocks. Long pale hair dangled over its face and halfway down its ribs.

'What's *that*?' Flax asked the dog-fae.

'It's a banshee,★ a very bad fairy from Ireland.'

'Then what's it doing here?'

'Haunting this mansion,' said the dog-fae.

★*Just because banshees are Irish, it doesn't mean they have to stay in Ireland.*

9. Flax Bribes a Banshee

'Woe!' wailed the banshee. 'Woe! Woe!'

'I'll give *you* woe if you don't stop,' said Flax. 'What's your name?'

The banshee peered through her long pale hair. 'My name is Biddy O'Fearon O'Flynn, darling. I was brought from the bogs of Ireland by O'Connor O'Grady O'Brien. He set me to haunt this place. I cannot leave until—'

'Don't call me darling. Call me Flax.
I'm a bad fairy.'

'Sure and you are!' Biddy sounded
admiring. 'Now I look at you properly,
I see you are a bit bad.'

'I'm *very* bad,' corrected Flax. 'I am
earning my Badge of Badness.'

The banshee turned to the dog-fae.
'Dog, dear, what is she talking about?'

'A Badge of Badness is a special award
that Certain Parties offer for bad fairies,'
said the dog-fae.

'What Certain Parties are those,
dog, dear?'

'The Head Hags of Hags' Abademy
of Badness.'

Flax pricked up her ears. She hadn't
known about the Abademy, which wasn't
surprising, since Maggie, Anni and Kirsty
had only just thought it up the day before.

'That sounds like a *school*,' she said.
'I don't want any awards from a *school*.'

'You want this one,' said the dog-fae.
'A Badge of Badness is proof that you are
a qualified Bad Fairy. Only the baddest of
the bad can have one. They will soon be
all the rage.'

'I want one too!' said Biddy. 'How do
I earn one, dog, dear?'

'You have to create and perform an act
of breathtaking badness,' said Flax.

Biddy wrung her hands. 'Woe! Woe!
How can I do that? I'm bound to this
tower until a child of the house of
O'Connor O'Grady O'Brien releases me!'

'You can't get a Badge of Badness then,'
gloated Flax. Then she narrowed her eyes.
'That is, unless you help me get mine.
Then I'll put in a bad word for you.'

'Would you do that for me, Flax?'

'We'll see,' said Flax. 'I have a stupid
human that I want you to keep locked up
in your tower. Don't let it out. It'll babble
about kidnappers and whine a lot. Ignore
it. Scare it. Bother it. Can you do that?'

'Indeed I can!' said Biddy. 'No one
bothers better than a banshee. Leave it
to me, Flax.'

Flax dragged the unconscious Dulcinea Sweet into the tower. 'Here it is,' she said, dumping the limp film star face down at the banshee's feet. *'Don't* let it escape.'

The kidnapping was done. Now Flax had to get the sparkly clip out of the stinging nettle before she could send a ransom demand.

If she could just get her hands on those kidnappers, she could make *sure* they got the blame. She had to get them here to the scene of the crime. Maybe she could put *them* into storage too!

Flax explored the mansion. The rooms upstairs were empty. The ground floor had dust, cobwebs and a rotting piano, but a trapdoor in the kitchen led to a cellar. Down there, Flax found a keg of pickled herrings. She ate some, then she left the mansion.

'Where to now?' asked the dog-fae.

'I have to get something from the school. Then I need those kidnappers. Find them for me.'

Without waiting for the fetch to answer, Flax leapt into the air. Her wings beat wildly. She flapped along, her rat-heeled boots just clearing the rocks and grass.

Back at the school, the teachers were trying to discover who had stolen the lunches. Flax got the sparkly clip out of the stinging nettle and pinned it in her hair. Next she stole a uniform from the school store and put it on. She stole a bag from the cloakroom and stuffed her overalls inside.

'You look like a human,' jeered the dog-fae, popping into view.

'That's the plan.'

'Is that a bug on your head?'

'No. It's that pink silly magic thing Dulcinea Sweet wears. If I have it, then the kidnappers will think I'm her. Then they will kidnap *me*, and *I* can kidnap *them*.'

The dog-fae landed on Flax's head, and sniffed hard at the clip. 'That's not magic. It's something made by humans.'

Flax squinted upwards. 'Get off my head. Where are the kidnappers?'

'They are circling the school in a pink van. Maybe they are homing in on that head-bug.'

'The only bug on my head is you. Get off. Get in the bag.' She shook her head hard, sending the dog-fae spinning.

'*Yrrrrr*,' snarled the dog-fae. 'You're *mince*, fairy!'

'Inside.' Flax pointed.

The dog-fae scrambled into the bag.

Flax went outside to the school gates to wait for the kidnappers. The dog-fae was right. The pink van was crawling along the street towards her. The trap was set. Now to get herself kidnapped.

10. The Kidnappers Make a Move

As the van approached, Flax waved her arms. The van stopped. A wispy-bearded face peered out the window at Flax.

Flax smiled. 'Are you the people my mama sent to take me somewhere safe?'

The face blinked. 'Um, just a minute,' it mumbled. It wound up the window and held a quick conversation with the other person inside the van.

Flax, being fairy breed, heard every word.

'Are you sure that's Dulcinea Sweet, Miffsy?' said the bearded one.

'Of course it's her!' said the one called Miffsy. 'She's wearing the transmitter. Can't you see it on her head?'

So, Flax realised, the magic clip that kept saying *Dulcinea Sweet is here* was called a transmitter. It was telling these kidnappers that *she* was Dulcinea Sweet.

'But the Sweet kid has longer hair,' protested the man with the beard.

'It's her,' said Miffsy. 'There's no way she'd let another kid wear a gift from her biggest fan.'

'I don't know, Miffsy. Sweet looks like a doll. This kid looks weird.'

'Film stars look different in real life. She probably cut her hair as a disguise.

It's definitely her. For sure. If Ma Sweet sent someone to get her, we'd better move fast.'

Winding the window down, the bearded kidnapper smiled. 'Miffsy and I have come to find Dulcinea Sweet. Are you really her?'

Flax patted her hair. 'Ooh, yes. I'm famous. Some horrible kidnappers are after me. Mama said to hide somewhere safe and not tell *anyone* except the people she sent to get me.'

'Hop into the van then,' said the man.

Flax looked doubtful. 'I'd better call Mama first. I have to tell her where I'm going to hide. If I don't tell her, nobody will know where we are!'

'Don't worry,' said the bearded man. 'We will call her when we get there, I promise you.'

'Um . . .' Flax pretended to consider. She thought that even the real Dulcinea Sweet wouldn't be silly enough to go off in a van with two strangers.

Miffsy got out of the van. She was even skinnier than Biddy Banshee. She scooped Flax up under one arm and tossed her into the van, then jumped back in the front seat. 'Drive on, Slick!' she urged the man with the beard.

The van puttered away. In the back seat, Flax smirked. They were soon out of the village, driving along the road that led to the mouldering mansion.

'I'm a famous film star,' she said. 'That's why the kidnappers want to get me.'

'We know you're famous,' said Miffsy, turning to look at her. She had a sharp nose and a voice like sour milk. 'We're big fans of yours, Slick and me.'

'Hey, Mister Slick, that's the place I
picked to hide in, right up ahead,' Flax
said. 'Everyone thinks it's haunted! The
kidnappers would be much too scared to
go there. Mama says they're really big
cowards. You won't be scared though,
will you? Just turn off the road here ...'

Slick spun the wheel. The van drove
into the stony lane, under the trees. 'It
looks pretty spooky,' Slick complained.

He parked in the shadows and got out, then looked hard at Flax. 'Is this place secret enough, do you think?'

'No one knows we're here except you and Miffsy and me.' Flax forced a tear out of her left eye. 'Mister Slick, will you stay with me? I'd be scared if I had to wait on my own.'

'Sure, kid.' Slick winked at Miffsy. 'Hear that, Miffs? The little film star wants our company!' He opened the door of the mansion. 'Inside, Dulcinea.'

Miffsy brought in supplies and Slick locked the door. He put the key in his pocket. 'Now we're all safe and sound, and no one will find us.'

Miffsy plinked on the rotting piano. Then she went into the kitchen and found the cellar. 'Just the place!' she called.

Slick took Flax by the arm. 'Come on!'

Flax let Slick take her into the kitchen, where Miffsy was halfway down the steps to the cellar. She went on down, and Flax and Slick followed. Slick closed the trapdoor.

Flax hugged Miffsy. 'Thank you!' she burbled. 'It's so *good* to be here!'

'Huh?' In the yellow lamplight, Miffsy looked puzzled.

'I'm safe! I'm safe!' squealed Flax, kicking her rat-heeled boots.

Miffsy peeled the fairy off her neck and laughed in a nasty way. 'That's where you're wrong, Dulcinea.'

'Safe!' Flax ran around, waving her arms.

Miffsy laughed again. 'Listen, Dulcinea. You've been kidnapped! Get it?'

'But you're my fans!' said Flax. 'Mama sent you!'

'We're fans of your money! And your mama didn't send us.' Miffsy pointed to the clip in Flax's hair. 'Remember the fan that sent you this sparkly clip? That was me. It's a very special clip. Inside it is a little transmitter that talks to my receiver in the van. That's how we tracked you down.'

'That's really bad magic.' Flax was impressed. Slick was silly but Miffsy was *so* bad that Flax almost wished she didn't have to ruin her plans.

'There's no such thing as magic, you stupid kid. It's electronics,' said Miffsy. 'So you're not safe. We tracked you and kidnapped you. No one knows where you are except for Slick and me. Now your mama is going to pay to get you back.'

11. Flax Arranges a Ransom

Flax stared, and clasped her hands.
'*You're* the kidnappers who were after
me before?'

'Yes!' snapped Miffsy. 'And now we've
got you.'

'Hurrah!' Flax did a handspring. Her
rat-heeled boots hit Miffsy's nose. 'Mama
said kidnappers were nasty. I like you,
though. If I stay with you, I can be your

little girl and never make films again!'

'But you have to make films,' said Slick. 'You're a film star. Film stars make films. Films make money.'

'Films are silly,' said Flax, dancing a jig. 'I want to live with you. We can kidnap people.'

Slick and Miffsy stared. 'Stop bouncing!' snapped Miffsy. 'You're kidnapped. You should be scared.'

'Let's call her mama right now,' said Slick. 'As soon as she pays the ransom, the kid can go home.'

'I want to stay here,' sang Flax. 'It's like camping!'

Miffsy shook her head. 'It's too soon. Her ma won't know the kid's missing yet. We have to give her time to get scared. You can't use our mobile phone either. The cops might trace it.'

Flax stopped dancing. 'I don't want to go home.'

'You have to,' said Slick.

'No.'

'Yes.'

Flax pouted. 'I'm hungry.'

'Feed her,' said Slick. 'It might shut her up.'

'She can feed herself,' said Miffsy.

Flax opened the bag of supplies and ate the lot.

'Hey!' said Slick, but it was too late.

'I'm still hungry! I want pickles and pears. I want cucumber. I want—'

Flax's yammering made Miffsy's head ache. 'All right!' she snapped. 'One of us will get more food, and steal a phone.'

While she and Slick argued about who was to go, Flax got the dog-fae out of her stolen school bag.

'I need some of that cat-wort you put in the Daisy Dormers' sugar-sip.'

The dog-fae snarled. It had not enjoyed the school bag.

'I need some cat-wort. You go with Slick or Miffsy and get it. *Fetch*!'

'I don't like them,' growled the dog-fae.

'Go, or I'll squish you through the keyhole.'

The dog-fae squinted at Flax and decided she meant it. It sneaked across the floor and crawled into Miffsy's bag. Flax saw its eyes glaring through the cloth as Miffsy, who had lost the argument, left the cellar.

Flax chattered the whole time Miffsy was away. She kept telling Slick all about her grand life as a film star. Flax didn't know how films are made, but neither did Slick, so that was all right. She went on and on until his ears hurt.

An hour later Miffsy returned with the shopping and a stolen phone. 'I'll call her mama *now*,' Slick said. 'This kid's driving me nuts.'

He called Mama Sweet, jamming his finger in one ear to shut out the sound of Flax eating a cucumber dipped in pickles.

'Mama Sweet? Listen. We got your kid.

Sure it's her. Wears a nice pink clip. I said, *listen*! Take a big bag of money to—um—' He held the phone against his side and clicked his fingers at Flax. 'Where can we get your mama to leave the ransom money?'

'There's an old pink barn just outside the village,' said Flax, remembering what the dog-fae had told her.

'Take the money to the old pink barn outside the village tomorrow morning at six,' said Slick into the phone. 'Leave it there. No cops. When we get the money, you get the brat.' Slick handed the phone to Flax. 'Talk to your mama, Dulcinea. No tricks, or we'll leave you here forever.'

'Mama?' Flax whimpered. 'We're hiding out at—'

Slick grabbed the phone back. 'Pay up, or you never see your little film star again!'

He dropped the phone into the barrel of pickled herrings.

'We're going to be rich!' he told Miffsy.

That's what he thinks, said Flax to her third yellow pear.

The kidnappers talked about their plans for Mama Sweet's money. Flax finished her pear and licked her fingers. She sprinkled cat-wort over a treacle and chocolate cake, gave it to the kidnappers and then ate six bananas.

The kidnappers kept talking, stopping often to yawn halfway through their sentences. Flax shared the last ripe pear with the dog-fae. By the time they'd finished, the cat-wort cake had put the kidnappers to sleep.

'Let's go,' Flax told the dog-fae, wiping her sticky fingers on Slick's sleeve. 'We have a ransom to collect.'

She fished the stolen phone out of the herrings and cleaned it on Miffsy's shirt. Then she gathered the leftover food and clambered out of the cellar. She pushed the rotting piano into the kitchen and parked it on top of the trapdoor.

'Take me to this pink barn,' she told the dog-fae.

'You'll never be able to fly after all that food,' said the fetch. 'But it isn't far. We'll walk.'

Leaving the mouldering mansion behind them, the bad fairy and the dog-fae set off for the old barn. Flax's rat-heeled boots jigged with glee and the dog-fae waggled its furry tail as it perched on her shoulder. 'It's a pity I hate you so much,' said Flax. 'Otherwise we'd make a very bad team.'

'*Rrrrrr,*' said the dog-fae.

They arrived at the old pink barn well before dawn and climbed into the rafters to lie in wait for Mama Sweet. 'What are you going to do with this ransom?' asked the dog-fae.

'Nothing,' said Flax. 'I only want it so no one else can have it.'

The dog-fae looked impressed. 'Taking what you don't want, just so someone else can't have it is *bad*. You're bound to get your Badge of Badness now.'

'Of course I will,' said Flax.

12. Dancing on the Piano

Flax yawned. It was almost six o'clock in the morning and a lot had happened in the day-and-a-quarter since she had left the Academy of Sweetness.

'Here we go,' said the dog-fae, as Mama Sweet arrived with a big bag. She put it down inside the barn and got out a mobile phone. She tapped her foot. 'Come *on!*' she muttered. 'Call me!'

Flax, who was still in the rafters, pushed buttons on Miffsy's stolen phone until Mama Sweet's phone played a little tune.

'Mama!' Flax copied Dulcinea's voice.

'Dulcie, dear!' gasped Mama Sweet. 'Where are you?'

Flax grinned. 'Have you put the bag of money in the pink barn?'

'Of course I have! Where are you?'

'Get away from the barn right now,' said Flax. 'Slick and Miffsy will come for the ransom in their van. If they see anyone near the barn, they'll never let me out. Now please, Mama, do what they want. Go away, quickly.'

'Dulcinea . . . where are you?'

'Just go!'

Mama Sweet looked longingly at the bag of money. Then she left the barn.

Flax scooted down from the rafters and snatched the ransom.

The dog-fae giggled. 'Have you finished your act of Breathtaking Badness?'

'Not yet.' Flax waited a while and made another call to Mama Sweet.

'Hello? Dulcinea? Dulcinea, my dear, where are you?'

'I'm still locked in!' whined Flax.

'But *where*?' Mama Sweet sounded worried. 'I just paid a lot of money to get you back. We have to get started on your next film. Remember what your agent said, dear. Soon you'll be too old for little-girl fairy roles, and you can't act well enough for more dramatic roles. You must make lots of films while you can.'

Flax sobbed. 'All you—(*gasp*)—care about—(*gulp*)—is money!'

'That's not fair . . .' began Mama Sweet.

She sounded just a bit guilty as she added, 'I'm thinking about your future.'

Flax tossed the phone across the barn and scrambled onto the roof. She ripped a hole in her uniform shirt to let her wings out, and fluttered down. Her rat-heeled boots kicked joyfully as she skimmed along, clasping the ransom to her chest. The dog-fae whirred beside her.

When she reached the mouldering mansion she tramped into the kitchen.

In the cellar below, Slick and Miffsy were awake and blaming one another for losing their victim.

'You shouldn't have gone to sleep, Miffsy! Get the phone out of the herrings!'

'It's not there! And you went to sleep first!'

'That greedy kid must have—'

Flax sprang onto the rotten piano and jumped on the keys. The cacophony made the kidnappers in the cellar shout with terror.

Flax danced up and down. She didn't bother to cast a spell. The weight of the piano would keep the trapdoor shut until someone moved it away.

She got down on the floor and put her mouth to the trapdoor. *'Pssst!'*

'Who's there?' called Miffsy.

Flax laughed. 'It's me, Dulcinea Sweet,' she lied.

'How did you—oh, never mind. Let us out!'

'No chance,' said Flax. 'You kidnapped me. Now I have kidnapped you. Call Mama. You'll have to use your own phone, not the one Miffsy stole. Tell her you got the ransom from the barn.'

'But we *didn't*!' said Slick. 'We've been shut up here in the cellar!'

'Well, someone got it,' gloated Flax. 'You call Mama, and say it's been collected. Do it *now*.'

Slick made the call while Flax danced gleefully on the piano.

'Now, let us out,' demanded Miffsy.

'No!' said Flax. 'You might grab me again. Call somebody to come and move the piano, then you can get out. Of course, everyone will know you got tricked by a little girl.'

The kidnappers had two choices. They could stay in the cellar and eat pickled herrings forever or they could confess where they were and be let out.

13. Bad Deeds Gone ~~Wrong~~ Right

Flax left the kidnappers to think about it and went to see how Dulcinea Sweet was dealing with the banshee. She was about to bang on the door when she heard something that made her hair prickle.

'So, if I clasp my hands and take tiny steps all in a rush, it will look as if I'm floating?'

Flax had heard Dulcinea Sweet sound

boastful, frightened and bored. Now she sounded interested . . .

'That's it, girl, dear,' answered the banshee. ' 'Tis the sweep of the skirts that gives the illusion.'

'I *see*! Oh, Biddy, I've learned more from you than from any acting coach ever! When my agent sees what I can do now, he'll forget about silly little fairy films.'

Flax's lip lifted in a silent snarl. She kicked the door in and stormed into the tower. Here, she saw a horrible sight. Dulcinea and Biddy had been eating a meal of shamrock cake and clover cordial. The banshee looked plumper and her hair was neatly braided. Dulcinea had changed too. Her face no longer looked like a plastic doll's. It was bright and alert.

Dulcinea smiled at Flax. 'Oh, hello, Flax,' she said. 'Biddy and I have—'

Flax ignored Dulcinea. '*You*!' she snapped at Biddy. 'Call yourself a *banshee*?'

Biddy cringed. 'Now . . . I just—'

'I store a human with you and what do I find?'

'She's still here,' said Biddy.

'*Still here!* Fine! But is she *shaking and shrieking*? Is she *cringing and begging*? Is she *moaning and whining*? *Is* she?'

'No.'

'Have you bothered her *at all*?'

'No, Flax.'

'And *you* expect *me* to help *you* get a *Badge of Badness*!' said Flax. She pointed her sharpest fingernail at Biddy. 'If you mention *any* of this to *anyone* . . . I'll *tell the hags at the Abademy* what you did! You'll never get your Badge of Badness.' She whirled to face Dulcinea. 'And as for you! Your mama is *so* mad with you.'

'Who cares?' Dulcinea patted the
banshee on the shoulder. 'She won't stay
mad when she sees what Biddy taught
me. I'll make proper films now!' She
clasped her hands and took tiny steps.
She *did* look as if she was floating. 'Guess
what?' she said to Flax. Her eyes shone.

'Biddy is going to come and live with me. She's going to coach me in acting. She's—'

'You are so stupid!' interrupted Flax. 'Biddy can't go *anywhere*. She's stuck here in this mouldering mansion until a child of the house of O'Connor O'Grady O'Brien releases her.'

'Oh, that's all right, Flax, dear,' said Biddy. 'Dulcinea and I have had a long talk . . .'

Biddy chattered on, and Flax spun on her rat-heels and stormed down the stairs and out of the mouldering mansion. She was so angry she could hardly speak. Her wonderfully brilliantly breathtakingly bad deed had gone *wrong*.

'You might still get the Badge of Badness,' said the dog-fae. 'You *meant* badly.'

'I failed,' said Flax. Her wings drooped.

'I'll have to go back to Miss Kisses' Academy.'

The dog-fae knew Flax was right. She had done a lot of bad deeds, but somehow, the results had *not* been bad. Sadly, it buzzed away to report to the hags.

14. Seal of Sweetness

Flax tried to sneak back into the Academy, but Butterfly Cloudsinger caught her as she climbed through the window.

'Flax!' She clasped her hands. 'Oh, Flax, you sweet, sweet fairy! We found out about all your sweet deeds from Miss Kisses' Fairy-Reporter. Guess what? Miss Kisses is *soooo* pleased with you. You're going to get a *Seal of Sweetness*!'

'But—' Flax looked desperately about for the dog-fae, but it was in the cellar, reporting to the hags.

Miss Kisses swept in and pointed her wand at Flax. '*I* know a little fairy who has been out and about doing sweet deeds!' she simpered. 'I wonder who that little fairy might be? Um ... might her name be *Flax Lilykicker*?'

'I *didn't*!' snapped Flax, but Miss Kisses just laughed.

'Oh, but you did! It's all there in my Fairy-Reporter. Thanks to *you*, Flax, a little film star discovered her true talent. Thanks to *you*, one mama now knows her little girl is more important than money. Thanks to *you*, two kidnappers learned a lesson. Thanks to you, a lonely banshee found a friend. What's more, she has escaped her mouldering prison! Thanks—'

'Wait a minute!' Flax broke in. 'That banshee can't get out of the tower until a child of the house of O'Connor O'Grady O'Brien releases her!'

'That has happened and it's all thanks to a little fairy who thought she was bad!'

'But . . . but . . .' stammered Flax.

Miss Kisses widened her eyes. 'Can it be that she doesn't *know*?' she wondered aloud. 'Can Flax Lilykicker be unaware that Dulcinea Sweet's *real* name is Dulcinea O'Connor O'Grady O'Brien?'

'But—!'

Miss Kisses laughed. 'Dulcinea Sweet is a stage name, Flax. Her mama made it up because it sounded *sweet*. Dulcinea's great, great, great, great uncle O'Connor was the mad Irishman who built the mouldering mansion. Dulcinea is the last of the family.'

Flax kicked the ground. Her rat-heeled boots seemed to be turning fuzzy and pink. She could feel the tide of sweetness sneaking over her. The bag of ransom money was making her shoulders ache. After all, what use was human money* to a fairy?

Flax couldn't believe how many good deeds she had done by accident. She was a failure as a bad fairy.

'So,' said Miss Kisses. 'All's sweet that ends sweetly, and now a little fairy has earned her Seal of Sweetness.'

Flax sighed.

Then suddenly she had a brainwave. 'Miss Kisses, I never expected to earn a Seal of Sweetness,' she said slowly.

*Human money can be used only to buy human goods. The fairy breed have other ways of getting things.

A bad idea was dawning. 'I'd like to share my feelings with the rest of the little fairies. I want to say thank you to everyone by giving a party in the Pink Pavilion!'

'A party!' squealed Butterfly. She twirled around. 'Daisy Dormers, listen! Flax Lilykicker is giving a *party*!'

'A party,' said the dog-fae, popping into view as soon as Miss Kisses and Butterfly had flitted off. 'You didn't get your badge,' it added. 'The Head Hags had to turn you down.'

Flax shrugged. She had known that really, but it still hurt. 'It was a stupid idea, anyway.'

'I suppose a party will cheer you up,' said the dog-fae.

'I'm sure it will,' said Flax. She held out her hand. 'Come on, Fetch. Badge or no badge, we're going shopping.'

15. Flax Hosts a Party

Flax spent the whole ransom on human junk food. She bought a truck full of pink potato chips, and packets and packets of pink sugar cakes. She bought pink marshmallows, pink fizzy cordial and imported pink sugared popcorn and pink pies. She blackmailed an ogre to carry the food back to the Academy of Sweetness.

'Flax! Where have you *been*?' cried the

Daisy Dormers. 'We've been waiting for your party! Miss Kisses is going to present you with your Seal of Sweetness!'

'Follow me to the Pink Pavilion,' said Flax, leading the way. 'Be my guests!'

A minute later, twelve fairies and Miss Kisses were daintily gobbling Flax's party food. Flax stamped about in her rat-heeled boots, offering plates and packets and smiling sweetly.

An hour later, twelve pink frilly frothy fairy frocks and one elegant pink silken robe burst at the seams, and thirteen fairy faces broke out in spots. Junk food is bad for humans. It's really, *really* bad for good fairies.

Flax was considering the marvellous mess when the dog-fae buzzed up and nipped her on the ear.

'Flax, you're wanted.'

'Go away.'

'All right. If you don't *want* a Badge of Badness ...'

'*What*?' Flax spun round. 'But ... but I *failed*! You said I did. All my bad deeds went *wrong*.'

'Not this one!' The dog-fae flicked its tail at the room of moaning spotty fairies.

'You've put this lot out of action for at least a week. That will give the humans a break from all those sweet deeds.'

'Aye,' said Kirsty Breeks, striding into the Pink Pavilion in a swirl of tartan tatters. 'It will give humans a chance to do some good for themselves, if they've a mind to!' She took Flax by the hand. 'Come along, Flax Lilykicker. You are invited to a special presentation. You will become the very first fairy to be inducted into the Abademy Hall of Badness.'

The dog-fae giggled at Flax. 'A special presentation? A Badge of Badness to go with your Seal of Sweetness? What kind of fairy gets both on the same day?'

Flax grabbed the fetch out of the air. She put it in her pocket, and buttoned down the flap with her free hand. 'A bad one,' she said firmly. 'That's what.'

'You're *mince*, fairy!' snarled the dog-fae, 'I hate you.' But inside the pocket its fuzzy tail was waggling.

Flax patted the pocket and looked up at Kirsty Breeks. 'The two of us are ready,' she said. 'Where are the rest of the hags?'

A Note from Tiffany Mandrake

Psst, this is me, Tiffany Mandrake, again. The Abademy of Badness has been running for a while now. It's close to where you live.

I live in the grounds. The Hags know I'm here, and they trust me completely.

They know I'll never say a word . . . and I haven't . . . except to you.

About the Author

Bad behaviour is nothing new to Tiffany Mandrake—some of her best friends are Little Horrors! And all sorts of magical visitors come to her cosy, creepy cottage in the grounds of the Hags' Abademy.

Tiffany's favourite creature is the dragon who lives in her cupboard and heats water for her bath. She rather hopes the skunk-fae doesn't come to visit again, for obvious reasons.

About the Artist

Martin Chatterton once had a dog called Sam, who looked exactly like a cocker spaniel . . . except she was much smaller and had wings. According to Martin, she even used to flutter around his head and say annoying things. Hmmm!

Martin has done so many bad deeds he is sure he deserves several Badges of Badness. 'Never trust a good person' is his motto.